Mitchell Foy

Stay Wildly

Jurassic!

Mitchell Foy is a 19-year-old young man who created this book in his graphic arts class In high school. Mitch was diagnosed with autism at the age of 5. This has never held Mitch back from passing all MCAS exams, graduating high school and writing a children's book. Mitchell lives with his parents and older brother, David.

T-REX AND ME

by Mitchell Foy

AUSTIN MACAULEY PUBLISHERS™

LONDON • CAMBRIDGE • NEW YORK • SHARJAH

Copyright © Mitchell Foy (2021)

Ordering Information
Quantity sales: Special discounts are available on quantity purchases by corporations, associations, and others. For details, contact the publisher at the address below.

Publisher's Cataloging-in-Publication data
Foy, Mitchell
T-Rex and Me

ISBN 9781649793270 (Paperback)
ISBN 9781649793287 (Hardback)
ISBN 9781649793294 (ePub e-book)

Library of Congress Control Number: 2021915069

www.austinmacauley.com/us

First Published (2021)
Austin Macauley Publishers LLC
40 Wall Street, 33rd Floor, Suite 3302
New York, NY 10005
USA

mail-usa@austinmacauley.com
+1 (646) 5125767

My book is dedicated to my teacher, Brian Trainer of Whittier Tech high school. He is my mentor and also my friend.

(The Story of a Tyrannosaurus Rex and Me) (Dinosaur Man)

While out for a walk, I was admiring the environment. Taking pictures and nothing else. But then, I heard a ferocious roar from out of nowhere that made me shiver! But I decided to keep on walking and ignore what I had heard.
I was gonna sit down and rest 'cause I was so tired, but just when I was ready to sit down, I saw huge footprints on the ground next to me.
"Cheese n crackers!" I shouted. Then I began to think, Is there a dinosaur around here?
When I first saw those footprints, it seemed like the footprints of the world's deadliest carnivorous killer, the Tyrannosaurus Rex!
I began to shake and think that if I hid in the forest, maybe it won't see or find me. But I started to think that tyrannosaurs have an incredible sense of smell; it could smell me from over half a mile away and I would be dead already.

I started to think when I kept on walking. Is there really a dinosaur in this forest, or maybe my eyes were just playing tricks on me? Would I forever be known as the boy who cried dinosaur? HaHaHa! But then, it happened. I was almost ready to get out of here and get back home when I saw something moving behind the trees; it had a long, huge tail, sharp teeth, tiny arms, and long muscular legs. I stopped, looked up, and suddenly when it came out of the forest, there she was; a ferocious, enormous tyrannosaurus rex.

I saw the rex, and she saw me. She was so close to me that she snorted on my face and blew my hat right off my head. I never realized how close I was to that prehistoric carnivore, but then I remembered what I said to myself, 'stay still, no noise, and hopefully it won't eat me or see me.'

And so she walked on and went on her way. But when she left, I decided to follow her and see where she would take me.

I kept following her and what I saw made me go crazy! I saw a dinosaur landscape full of dinosaurs.

It was like a secret, a hidden miracle I had never seen before.
My whole life I wanted to see dinosaurs. I had to search for the T-rex and did,
I kept on walking and walking, but then all of a sudden, I heard a screech from
out of nowhere. That sounded like a velociraptor. I knew I should be on the
lookout because velociraptors are aggressive, carnivorous pack hunters who
can run at speeds up to 40mph and 60 kph on two legs.
Standing 3ft tall and 6ft long and can weigh up to 20—30 pounds, and like
wolves, they hunt in packs and have an extremely sensitive sense of smell only
at night; they have a very tough brain called the olfactory bulb that helps
them smell better than a human or a dog. That's not a reptilian Phoenix I
want to run into when I'm in a forest. So I didn't worry about seeing all the
dinosaurs, I was worried about them eating me. A brachiosaurus may look
huge and tall but no fear, it's a herbivore.

Just then, I saw some bushes moving and rustling, and I heard a growling and snarling sound. I was shaking and shivering, and terrified by that sound. After the noise stopped, I started to continue to walk. But suddenly from out of nowhere, Boom! Out of the bushes there came raptors!

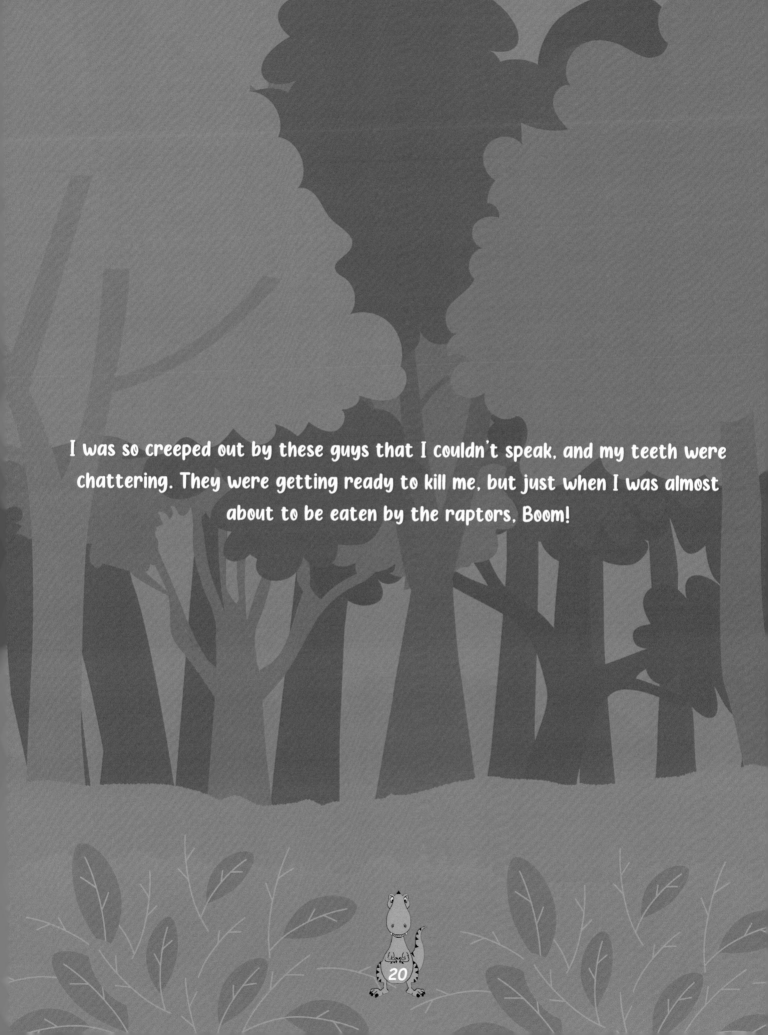

I was so creeped out by these guys that I couldn't speak, and my teeth were chattering. They were getting ready to kill me, but just when I was almost about to be eaten by the raptors, Boom!

The T-rex came back and saved my life.
After when she saved me from the raptors, she looked down at me with her
big eyes, came close to me, and I started to make contact with her.

When I made contact with her, I turned my head, reached out my hand slowly, and made sure she'd let me pet her. When I made contact with her, I was so surprised and shocked by what had happened. It seemed like she and I were like old friends and not enemies to each other.

When she and I became best friends, we realized the day was ending so I climbed up onto her and rode off into the sunset, riding on the magnificent beast!
The Queen of the Dinosaurs!
"Tyrannosaurus Rex!"

I woke up, went downstairs, and told my family the coolest dream
I ever had.
"You guys, I had the coolest dream, I dreamt that I saw a T-rex, and she
and I became best friends."
When I told my family about my dream, we all laughed for the rest
of the day!

The End